3/2000

"And in conclusion," Dr. Shtickle announced at the World Planetary Conference, "the reason the Red Planet is red is—" The audience burst out laughing. Then, last summer . . .

They came from outer space.
They landed in Minnesota.
They were . . .

TOMATOES
FROM
MARS

STORY BY ARTHUR YORINKS
PICTURES BY MORT DRUCKER

MICHAEL DI CAPUA BOOKS

HARPER COLLINS PUBLISHERS

FOR S. AND A., WITH LOVE   A.Y.

FOR KATIE, MEGAN, AND ALEX   M.D.

DESIGNED BY SUSAN MITCHELL

FIRST EDITION, 1999

As mankind innocently slept, the tomatoes moved silently toward Minneapolis.

No town or village was spared their hallmark red stain.

The population panicked.

In defense of the human race, some people threw rocks, or chairs, or anything they could get their hands on. But the tomatoes, impervious to pain, kept on coming.

"It's no use," cried the Mayor. "Run for your lives!"

As the tomatoes made a mess of Minneapolis, even more tomatoes were landing. There were sightings all across the country. Was this the end of civilization as we know it?

But one scientist was working even harder.
"If only we could communicate with the tomatoes," Dr. Shtickle
told his niece, Sally. "I know we could end this madness."

Meanwhile, at the White House, the President was desperate. "What are we going to *do*!"

"How about the Marines, sir?" someone suggested. Just then the phone rang.

It was Shtickle. He had a plan.
"Uh-huh," said the President. "I see," said the President. "Let's do it!" said the President. Shtickle's plan was put into motion.

Highly trained pilots were sent aloft to fill the sky with symbols of welcome. There was Man. There was Woman. There was Tomato.

It didn't work.

"Get me Shtickle!" said the President.

"No, no!" said Shtickle. "The entire earth will be covered in sauce. You've got to give me more time."

"Twelve hours, Shtickle. And then we blast them."

"We're doomed," said Shtickle. "Still, the tomatoes must have a weakness. But what is it? *What is it?*"

"Uncle," said Sally. "You can't think on an empty stomach."

"Oh, I'll just have a little salad," Shtickle said.

"Coming right up," said Sally. "Now, what kind of dressing would you like?"

"It doesn't matter, Sally, I'll— Wait! What did you say?"

"What kind of dressing would you like?"

"I've got it!" Shtickle shouted.

Suddenly Sally screamed. "Uncle! Look! The tomatoes are coming! The tomatoes are coming!" The tomatoes were coming.

Shtickle rushed to the pantry and began filling a shpritzer.

Then, as the Martian fruits came crashing through . . .

SHPRIIIIITZ!

Shtickle shpritzed them with extra virgin olive oil, red wine vinegar, fresh basil, and a little pinch of garlic. The tomatoes stopped, shook, shimmied. And scrammed!

When Dr. Shtickle's breakthrough was announced, everybody started shpritzing the invaders. Yes, the tomatoes cut quite a groove retreating to their home planet. Earth was saved!

And Shtickle? At a lavish **White House** ceremony, **Dr. Shtickle** was awarded the **Red Badge of Courage**. And henceforth his planetary theories, including the one about the onion rings of Saturn, were taken quite seriously.